Praise for **Gail Anderson-Dargatz**

For the Claire Abbott Mystery series
"[Claire] is a relatable character, and her psychic ability grows at just the right pace for a short series opener. For new adult readers who prefer hi-lo books and reluctant or struggling teen readers."
—*School Library Journal*

"Black forests, snowy weather and a growing sense of dread stir the pot of fear and tension to a deadly twister resulting in drastic action, last second rescue and several red faces among the town's male protectors of the peace. A sleuth with an edge launches Claire Abbott into a new series."

—*Canadian Mystery Reviews*

"A mad dash from start to finish, this latest entry in the Rapid Reads series is great for people who crave excitement."

—*Kirkus Reviews*

For *The Spawning Grounds*
"Writing as fluid as the river that runs through the story… A master storyteller, Anderson-Dargatz sets out with a tale of the familiar and seamlessly takes the reader where they never imagined they could go."

—*The Toronto Star*

D0376661

"The Canadian novelist writes what's sure to be classic literature."

—*The Huffington Post*

"Sharp imagery and spare dialogue are put to good use in Gail Anderson-Dargatz's ghost tale of a mysterious force intent on destroying a family in rural British Columbia."

—*The Globe and Mail*

For *A Recipe for Bees*
"In language remarkable for its suppleness and unforced simplicity, Anderson-Dargatz delivers both a quirky love story and a serene meditation on endurance and its rich rewards."

—*The Washington Post*

"A bravura work that in several ways recalls Carol Shields' *The Stone Diaries*. What Gail Anderson-Dargatz has achieved is a commemoration of a lifestyle and a collection of characters that live on when the novel is finished."

—*The Times Literary Supplement* (London)

For *From Scratch*
"Cookie's perseverance through hardship is certainly inspiring, and her bonds with the local community heartwarming."

—*Booklist*

No Return Address

No Return Address

Gail Anderson-Dargatz

ORCA BOOK PUBLISHERS

Library and Archives Canada Cataloguing in Publication

Anderson-Dargatz, Gail, 1963–, author
No return address / Gail Anderson-Dargatz.
(Rapid reads)

Issued in print and electronic formats.
ISBN 978-1-4598-1858-3 (softcover).—ISBN 978-1-4598-1859-0 (PDF).—
ISBN 978-1-4598-1860-6 (EPUB)

I. Title. II. Series: Rapid reads
PS8551.N3574N6 2018   C813'.54   C2017-907674-4
C2017-907675-2

First published in the United States, 2018
Library of Congress Control Number: 2018933739

Summary: In this short novel, a woman mourning the loss of her mother
gets a mysterious package in the mail. (RL 3.3)
A free reading guide for this title is available at rapid-reads.com.

*Orca Book Publishers is dedicated to preserving the environment and has
printed this book on Forest Stewardship Council® certified paper.*

Orca Book Publishers gratefully acknowledges the support for its publishing programs
provided by the following agencies: the Government of Canada through the Canada
Book Fund and the Canada Council for the Arts, and the Province of British Columbia
through the BC Arts Council and the Book Publishing Tax Credit.

Design by Jenn Playford
Cover images by iStock.com

ORCA BOOK PUBLISHERS
orcabook.com

Printed and bound in Canada.

21 20 19 18 • 4 3 2 1

For my sister Lynda

ONE

THAT THURSDAY MORNING, I woke up feeling sad. It was exactly one year since my mother had died. The sun was shining. The lilac bushes in my front yard were in bloom. It was one of those June mornings that usually puts a spring in my step. But my sorrow only deepened as the morning wore on.

I tried to shake the feeling on my daily walk down to the village. I took in the cloudless blue sky and breathed in the scent of the wild roses growing along the rural road. But that didn't help. By the time I reached the post office I felt real grief.

I must have looked sad too. As I pushed through the door the postal clerk asked, "You okay, Rhonda? Something wrong?"

"I'm fine," I told Susan. "Just a little tired, I guess."

I dodged more questions by opening my mailbox. Then I sorted my mail at the small counter, putting most of it in the recycling bin. Other than bills and advertising flyers, I didn't get much mail anymore. People sent emails from their computers instead. Going for the mail was mostly an excuse to get out of the house.

My mother used to send me letters, though, even after I moved to this lakeside village where she lived. She said emails were impersonal, just words on a screen. Handwritten letters, on the other hand, were a gift. I didn't understand why she kept sending me letters when I lived just up the road. But now that Mom had passed away, I missed getting them.

As I thought of my mother's letters, a new wave of grief washed over me. But I didn't want to cry in front of the postal clerk. I wiped my eyes and tried to focus on sorting my mail.

Then I came across a delivery-notice card. A package had arrived in the mail for me. That was strange. I hadn't ordered anything online.

My birthday wasn't until fall, so I knew the parcel wasn't from my aunt. And in any case, Auntie Lisa lived in the area. She would just bring her gift over to my place. My brother, Doug, also had a house close by, but I hadn't seen him since Mom's funeral. Mom had been the one to bring our family together, for Sunday dinner at her condo.

I handed the delivery-notice card to the postal clerk. Susan paused as she took it. "Are you sure you're okay?" she asked.

I shrugged. "I just realized it's one year today since my mother died."

"Oh, honey, I'm so sorry." Susan squeezed my hand. "I loved your mom! Meg was such a dear woman. We talked here just about every day."

In her final years my mom had lived in a condo only a couple of blocks from the post office. After my marriage ended I rented a house just up the road from her. I was glad I did. Mom had retired from her teaching job. She often took care of my son when he was too young to stay at home alone. And when Mom got the news from her doctor that she had breast cancer, I was there to help her out. As I thought of those final years with my mother, I started to tear up again.

"You and your mom were very close, weren't you?" Susan asked me.

I nodded. "She was always there for me," I said.

"I know you were a big help to her when she was sick."

"She helped me through a rough time too," I said.

"Your divorce?"

I hesitated before answering. I imagined my mother had told Susan about that. Mom wasn't always discreet. She sometimes told strangers, like Susan, about my life. Mom had also stuck her nose in my business, giving me advice even though I was a grown woman. But after her death, I would have given anything to have one last chat with her. I often wished for her guidance now, especially her tips on parenting my son, Cody.

"I don't know how I would have gotten through my divorce without her," I said. "She took care of Cody when I needed to deal with—" I stopped there. Now I was giving Susan too much information. I could see why my mother had befriended Susan though.

She *was* easy to talk to.

Susan waited a moment to see if I would continue. When I didn't, she waved the delivery notice. "I'll get your package," she said.

I took off my glasses and wiped my eyes as I waited. I was glad I was the only person in the post office. It had been a year since my mother's death. Why was I crying *now*?

"Here you go," said Susan. She set a small box on the counter in front of me.

"This can't be right," I said.

"Wrong address?" Susan asked.

"No, it's addressed to me. But this package is from my *mother*."

"That's impossible. Like you said, Meg has been gone a year." Susan peered at the box. "And why do you think it's from her? There's no return address."

I ran a finger along my own address, written on the brown wrapping. "I would know my mother's handwriting anywhere," I said.

I looked up at Susan. "Did she send this *before* her death? Could this package have been lost in the mail for that long?"

Susan scratched her head. "I suppose. Stranger things have happened. I once read about a letter that was delivered forty-five years after it was sent." She took a close look at the postmark. "But your package was mailed this week."

I felt a shock run through me. *Could* my mother have sent this parcel? Was she still alive? I shook my head at the foolish idea. When my mother passed away I was right there holding her hand. "I don't understand," I said. "Who sent this?"

Susan shrugged. "I guess you'll have to open it to find out." She looked down at the box as if she wanted to find out too.

While I liked Susan, I didn't know her that well. I wasn't about to open the package in front of her. Who knew what was inside?

Still, I couldn't wait until I got home. I carried the box back to the counter by the mailboxes. There I used my keys to rip the tape on the box. I tore off the brown paper wrapper and opened the flaps. "Oh!" I cried, because I couldn't believe what I found inside.

TWO

I WAS HOLDING a handwritten letter from my mother. Tears blurred my vision. This couldn't be happening. My mother had been gone a year. Who had sent this?

"What is it?" Susan asked. She had heard me cry out. "What's wrong?"

"Nothing," I said. "Everything's fine." That was a lie, of course. I tucked the letter back in the box and closed the flaps. I knew if I tried reading it here in the post office

I couldn't stop myself from crying. I had already embarrassed myself enough.

I kept my back to Susan as I stuffed the brown wrapping in the recycling bin. Then I picked up the box and hurried out the door.

"You take care," Susan called after me. She sounded concerned.

I held up a hand, but I didn't turn my head. My mind raced as I walked back up the country road. Why had my mother arranged to have this package sent to me a year after she died? Who had put it in the mail for her? The letter would have to be important. Otherwise, why would Mom go to such lengths to get it to me on the anniversary of her death?

When I got home I put the box down on the kitchen table. But I felt nervous now and didn't open it right away. Did Mom have a secret she had kept from me? Was the letter a confession of some kind?

I paced back and forth by the table for a bit.

Then I rearranged the bottles in the spice rack, lining them up neatly so their labels all faced outward. Cody had cooked supper the night before and put the bottles back in the wrong order. When I was anxious, little things like that really bugged me.

Finally, I sat at the kitchen table and opened the box. My hands shook as I took out the letter and read it.

My dearest Rhonda:

I know you think I'm very old-fashioned for writing letters. You're always telling me to send an email or text message instead. But we don't have Wi-Fi or cell service in the afterlife. Reception here is lousy.

I hope that small joke makes you smile rather than cry. I've developed a dark sense of humor now that I'm facing the end of my life. Yes, I am writing this just before my death. My doctor has told me I likely have only weeks to live. So, I'm wrapping up loose ends and making the most of every day.

First, I want to say that living close to you and Cody these past few years has meant everything to me. I loved being a teacher, but being a grandma to Cody was even more fun. I hope you know you gave me a gift on those days when you asked me to take care of him.

Then, when I got sick, you took care of me. You held my hand through my doctor's appointments and treatments. You and Cody made me meals when I didn't feel like eating. Cody cheered me up when I was feeling down. You took me to the cancer clinic and helped me pick out a wig. You applied my makeup so I'd feel pretty.

And you did all this just after your marriage had ended and as you started to rebuild your life. I hope that now, a year after my death, things have finally settled for you.

I have another favor to ask of you. In this box you'll find your brother's green yo-yo. I know you'll remember it from your childhood, as you often stole it from Doug's room. You tried and tried to do those yo-yo tricks that seemed to come so easily to Doug. Then you got mad at your brother when he showed you how to do them! You would have learned if you'd listened to your big brother. Maybe now that you're a grown-up you can let him teach you a trick or two?

Please take this yo-yo to your brother and hand it to him in person. Don't leave it on his doorstep or mail it to him. Don't even bother to phone ahead. Just knock on Doug's door when you know he's home, and hand him the yo-yo. That's not too much to ask, right? Or perhaps this task is too much to ask of my shy and stubborn daughter. Do it anyway. For me.

That's it for now.

I'll love you always. Hugs and kisses,

Mom

I put the letter down and wiped my eyes. Then I reached into the box and pulled out a wad of wrapping paper. Inside I found my brother's old yo-yo. It was pretty beat-up, but the string was still intact. I stood up and tried it out. It rolled down the string and back into my hand on the first try. Memories of watching my brother do his yo-yo tricks flooded back to me. He could do all kinds of fancy moves with the yo-yo, things I was never able to do.

I put the yo-yo on the table and read my mother's letter again. Mom's request didn't make sense. Why had she sent *me* the yo-yo? Why hadn't she just sent it to Doug? And why had she sent it to me on the anniversary of her death? I had expected the letter to be about something big. Instead it was about a yo-yo.

Then again, maybe the letter *was* about something important. Mom had been a teacher at the high school until she retired. She always said her real job was to help students figure things out for themselves. Maybe that's what she was up to here. But what did she want me to figure out?

I read the letter again, looking for clues. She had called me her "shy and stubborn daughter." I looked in the full-length mirror that hung by the kitchen door. My own sad face stared back at me. I had just turned forty. A few strands of gray hair stood out in my brown curls. Lines had formed at the corners of my eyes. I didn't bother to dress up or wear makeup, as I worked at home. I looked — what was the word Mom used to describe dull, timid women? *Mousy*.

Is *that* how my mother had seen me? I didn't think of myself as shy, but I *was* private. I kept to myself for the most part and worked from home, where I ran a bookkeeping service. Most of the time my only company was my teenage son, Cody. And he would head off to university in a year.

But stubborn? I'd never thought of myself as headstrong, or willful either. It *was* true that when Doug tried to teach me to use the yo-yo when I was a kid, I got mad. He was my older brother, always telling me what to do. That had bugged me. So, I tried telling *him* what to do. When we were kids, he called me bossy. But we were both grown-ups now. I wasn't like that around him anymore, was I?

I thought about that for a minute. The last time I had talked to Doug was at Mom's funeral. He had wanted to stand up in front of the attendees and tell everyone about the funny things Mom did. I told him I didn't want him to. It was a funeral, after all, and Mom's antics had often embarrassed me. When I was a kid she had once picked me up at school wearing a duck costume. She'd thought it would make the kids laugh, but I was humiliated! I had slid down in the car seat so the other kids wouldn't see me with her. But they all knew my mom.

When Doug told that story at the funeral, everyone laughed and looked at me. I slid down in the church pew, embarrassed again. At the funeral reception I had to smile politely as everyone made jokes about Mom's duck costume. Smiling was the last thing I wanted to do right then. My mother had just passed away. When Doug came up to me while I was in the church kitchen, I told him off. We hadn't spoken since.

Even before the funeral, though, things hadn't been all that good between my brother and me. We had been distant from each other since my divorce. My brother was still friendly with my ex-husband, Glen. I didn't like the fact that they still hung out together, especially when I rarely saw Doug anymore. I was also mad that Doug hadn't helped me with Mom's care after she got sick. But that didn't make me stubborn, did it?

I scanned the letter. What did Mom mean when she wrote *Maybe now that you're a grown-up you can let him teach you a trick or two?*

Did she really mean I should learn to play with this yo-yo? It was a child's toy.

I carefully folded Mom's letter and picked up the yo-yo again. I tried to do a trick called Rock the Baby, holding the string with both hands to make a triangle. The yo-yo was supposed to hang in the middle of the triangle and spin to look like a rocking cradle. But my fingers got all caught up in the string. I tried again, but I just couldn't get it. I wound up the string and put the yo-yo on Mom's letter.

I sat for a time in my neatly ordered kitchen, trying to make sense of her letter. I kept my house uncluttered because seeing everything in its place made me feel calm. But my tidy house didn't offer me peace of mind now. Even a year after her death, Mom was still meddling in my life. But what was she up to exactly?

THREE

I TRIED WORKING after I'd opened the package from my mother. But I couldn't focus on bookkeeping. The numbers just got jumbled in my head, and I kept making mistakes.

I finally gave up and organized the kitchen shelves. Then I tidied the bathroom and my bedroom. I vacuumed the living room floor, even though I'd just done that on Tuesday. I even did my son's laundry and made his bed, though I knew I shouldn't. He needed to do his own chores. In any case, he didn't like me messing with his things. Still, I couldn't help myself. I always cleaned house when I was upset.

When Cody got home from school I was back sitting at the kitchen table. My mother's letter was open in front of me.

"Hey," he said, closing the kitchen door behind him. "What's up, Mom? You okay? You look kind of out of it."

I shook my head to clear my thoughts. "I got a package today from Grandma," I said. "I'm just trying to sort out what her letter means."

"You got a letter from *Grandma*?" Cody dropped his backpack to the floor and took a seat at the table. "You're kidding me."

"No, for real. Look." I handed him the letter. He read it and then picked up the yo-yo. "Cool," he said. "My grandma's a zombie!"

"That's not funny," I said. "Be respectful." But I smiled nevertheless.

"Who really sent it?" Cody asked.

"I have no idea. There was no return address." I thought for a moment. "I suppose it could have been Doug. He and Mom might have been in on it together. Maybe it was their idea of a joke. I could see them cooking up something like this. Doug was always Mom's favorite."

Cody slung the yo-yo to the floor and spun it back up. "You don't really believe that, do you?"

"Doug is like Mom—a free spirit. He doesn't take life seriously any more than she did. He's well into his forties and he still races go-karts, for heaven's sake. He's always playing around like a kid." I shrugged. "I guess I took after Dad."

Cody gave me a look, like he didn't buy that. "You're more like Grandma than you think," he said. "Anyway, why would Uncle Doug mail his yo-yo to you? It makes no sense."

"None of this makes sense." I held out my hand, and Cody gave me back the toy. "Why would my mother send this yo-yo, of all things?" I held it for a moment, thinking of trying it out again. Instead I dropped it in the box. "I should forget the whole thing," I said. "Maybe I'll just toss this yo-yo into the attic with the rest of Mom's stuff."

Cody shook his head. "You *know* you have to deliver the yo-yo to Uncle Doug, Mom." He tapped the letter. "It was Grandma's last wish." Then he wiggled his fingers in my face and spoke with a spooky voice. "If you don't deliver the yo-yo to Uncle Doug, Grandma will haunt you!"

I gave him a gentle push to get him to stop. "But why *now*? Why a year after her death?"

"Who knows? Grandma was a little eccentric, always doing crazy things. Remember the time she covered herself in gray paint and pretended to be a statue by the art gallery? She stood so still she really looked like one too. People passing by freaked when she moved."

I laughed at the memory despite myself. "She sure did like to mess with people's minds," I said. I held up the letter. "Even mine."

"Nah. Grandma just wanted to make people laugh. She liked to shake them up a bit so they weren't so stiff." Cody held my eye for a moment, like he was talking about me. Then he grabbed the yo-yo again and spun it down. "Anyway, it's pretty clear what she's up to now."

"Oh?" I said.

He flicked the yo-yo back up. "Grandma wants you and Uncle Doug to talk to each other. *That's* why she wants you to deliver this yo-yo to him."

"We talk."

"You haven't seen Uncle Doug since Grandma's funeral. And you guys weren't exactly getting along before that."

I fidgeted with the letter. "I'm embarrassed that you noticed," I said.

"How could I *not* notice? You stopped visiting Doug, and he stopped coming over. I never see him anymore."

"Honey, families aren't like what you see on TV. Doug and I may have grown up together, but that doesn't mean we like each other now."

"Yeah, I know. But you and Uncle Doug *did* get along before you and Dad split up. Doug was over at our place all the time."

Cody was right. My ex-husband and my brother had been friends long before I married Glen. In fact, I had met Glen through my brother, at a party at Doug's place.

After Glen and I divorced my brother kept up his friendship with Glen. Like I said, that made me mad. No, that *hurt*. My brother went over to Glen's place but didn't come to ours. I felt like Doug had picked Glen over me. But *I* was Doug's sister.

"Uncle Doug used to take me fishing," Cody said. "We played games on my gaming console all the time. He was fun. I miss him."

I sat back to think about that. Was my resentment over Doug's friendship with Glen hurting my son? Was *I* stopping Cody from seeing his uncle? "I'm sorry that Doug and I aren't close anymore," I said. "I'm just not sure what to do about it."

Cody dropped the yo-yo in my hand. "Start by taking this over to Uncle Doug like Grandma asked. Work things out. Maybe then I can race go-karts with him again."

I eyed my son. "Did Grandma put *you* up to this? Are *you* the one who mailed this package?"

"No!"

I didn't think he was lying, but then, he was teenage boy. Only the week before he had eaten an entire frozen cake in one sitting. He'd then denied it, even though the crumbs were all over his T-shirt. And the cake container was sitting at his feet. And his mouth was covered in chocolate.

"I swear, Mom, it wasn't me," he said. "I didn't send Grandma's package to you."

"Well, it sure as heck wasn't my mother." I thought for a moment. "Then it must have been Lisa who sent it," I said. "Mom *would* have asked her to."

"And Auntie is the only one in our family crazy enough to do it," Cody said.

I laughed. "You may be right. They *were* sisters, after all." I tossed the yo-yo and caught it again. "I'm going to have a little chat with her," I said. I put the yo-yo and letter in the box. "You okay making supper for yourself? I think I'll head into town now to see her."

"Finally!" said Cody.

"What do you mean?"

Cody made a face like I should know exactly what he meant. "It's not just Uncle Doug you've been avoiding. You haven't seen Auntie Lisa for a while either, Mom."

I waved that off. "I've just been busy."

"No, you've been depressed."

I sat back. "I know I look sad today. It's the anniversary of my mother's death. It's only natural that I would feel down."

Cody shook his head. "No, you've been miserable for longer than that. Ever since Grandma died you've been keeping to yourself. You hardly go out anymore." He lowered his voice as if someone might hear. "And Mom, some days you don't brush your hair."

I glanced in the mirror by the kitchen door and patted my hair into place. "I've been trying to build my bookkeeping business," I said. "I work with most of my clients by email. I don't have to get dressed to go out."

"You've been hiding," said Cody.

"Hiding? From what?"

Cody shrugged. "You tell me, Mom."

I took a long look at my son. He was a smart kid, maybe too smart for my liking at the moment. He would graduate from high school the following year and then head to university. He was about to go off on his own to start his adult life. I knew that was for the best.

Still, the thought of him moving out made me feel lonely. My marriage had ended. My mother had died. I knew people in the community but couldn't think of anyone I wanted to share a pot of tea with. In that moment I realized just how lonely I was. My son was right. I had been sad for a long time. And I *had* been hiding, but from what?

"If you're going into town, will you stop at Uncle Doug's place too?" Cody asked.

"Can I come with you? I'd really like to see him again."

"I want to talk to Lisa about Mom's package first," I said. "I need to know what this is all about. Then maybe I'll take the yo-yo to Doug another day."

"Can I go with you to see him then?"

I paused to take in the look on my son's face. He really was missing his uncle. "We'll see," I said.

FOUR

I DROVE TO Lisa's place that evening. Both she and my brother, Doug, lived in the same town, a half-hour drive from my village. As Cody had said, I rarely visited her anymore. I had always gone to her place with my mother. I knew I should see more of her, but I just never got around to it.

Still, I sometimes felt I had more in common with my aunt than with my mother. Lisa was practical and sensible in a way my mother never was. She worked as an accountant, helping business owners make sense of their finances, their money matters. I also worked with numbers in my bookkeeping business.

I pushed the doorbell. Lisa opened the door. "Rhonda!" she said. "It's so good to see you!"

I held up the parcel from my mother. "Did you send this?" I asked.

My aunt laughed. "Well, hello to you too!"

I handed her the small box. "Did you?"

"What is it?" She opened it and pulled out the letter. "Oh!" she said when she realized who had written it. She tucked the box under her arm and read the letter as she walked down the hall.

I followed, closing the door behind me. "You *didn't* send it?" I asked.

"It's from your mother!"

"I know. But I only received it today, on the anniversary of her death. And the package was postmarked this week. Someone else must have sent it."

She peered at me over her glasses. "Well, it wasn't me."

"Who then?"

"How should I know?" She put the box on the table. "I was going to call you this evening. I knew it would be a hard day for you — for us both. She sighed. "Sit, and I'll make us tea."

She put the kettle on as I sat at the round kitchen table. Lisa must have just come home from work. She was still dressed in a navy-blue suit jacket and skirt. But she had kicked off her heels and put on a pair of pink bunny slippers.

"Mom didn't tell you she was sending that package before she died?" I asked.

"No! This is the first I've heard of it." Lisa pulled the yo-yo out of the box. "But this is so like her, isn't it?" She held up the toy. "Trust Meg to send you a yo-yo from beyond the grave."

"She wants me to deliver it to Doug," I said.

"I see that."

"Why didn't she just give it to him before she died? Or send it to him instead?"

"Oh, Rhonda, you know exactly why."

I nodded, but I couldn't look at her. "She wanted me to talk to Doug."

Lisa put the yo-yo in my hand and clasped both of hers around it. "She wanted you to mend things with your brother," she said. "And get over whatever hurt there is between you. Isn't it about time?"

I didn't answer. The thought of facing my brother made me uncomfortable. I just wasn't sure I was ready. I changed the subject. "Do you have any idea who might have put this box in the mail?"

Lisa shrugged. "Does it really matter who mailed it?"

"It matters to me." I paused. "I want to know who Mom trusted with this last wish. I was hoping it was you. You're her sister."

"And if it was someone other than me who sent the package on Meg's behalf?"

"Then Mom trusted that person more than me."

My aunt put her hand on my arm. "Oh, honey. Is that what you think?"

I waved the letter. "Here she is, trying to teach me one of her lessons. It's like —" I paused as I struggled to make sense of my feelings. "It's like I'm just another one of her students. And whoever sent this was closer to Mom than I was."

"And that hurts."

I nodded, staring down at the letter. When she said the words out loud, I realized how childish they sounded. But that was how I felt. "After the divorce I only had Mom and Cody," I said to explain myself. "Now I only have Cody. I don't have any friends."

"Have you tried to make any?"

"Making friends is much harder when

you're older and have a kid," I said. "I don't have time to meet new people."

"Well, you'll just need to make the time." Lisa got up and made tea, and then carried the teapot and cups to the table.

"You think it was Doug who sent the package for Mom?" I asked. I hesitated. "Was Mom closer to him than me?"

Lisa didn't answer right away. She went to the fridge for a small jug of milk. Her silence made me feel unsure of myself.

"Doug didn't help out at all when Mom was sick, you know," I said. "I was there for every one of Mom's doctor's appointments."

My aunt sat in the chair right beside me so she could wrap an arm around my shoulders. "Listen, I can't tell you who sent that package. But I *can* tell you what really matters here." She tapped the letter. "Meg can't be here anymore, so she wants you and Doug to be there for each other." She paused. "And for Cody.

I pulled away. "I'm always there for Cody," I said.

"Of course, you are," Lisa said. "But Cody needs men in his life too."

"He sees his father. He stays with Glen every second weekend."

"From what you've told me, Glen has started a new family. That's got to be hard on Cody."

"It is. Cody isn't Glen's main focus now. His wife and new baby are. Cody says he often feels like an outsider when he goes there." I swallowed hard. I still felt jealous that Glen had a new family, even though we'd been divorced for several years now.

"Rhonda, Doug could offer Cody a lot. The boy could use an uncle, especially now." My aunt smiled. "I'd like to think I've offered you a fair amount over the years."

I took Lisa's hand. "You have."

She had helped me start my bookkeeping

business. She'd sent clients my way and given me advice. That had meant a lot, especially when my mother couldn't understand why I wanted to be a bookkeeper. She'd thought it was a dull job. But I liked working with numbers. I could make sense of them. That was comforting. Especially when the rest of my life was so often chaotic and messy.

"Cody wants to go with me to Doug's place when I deliver the yo-yo," I said.

"Maybe this first visit should be between you and your brother. You don't want Cody listening in as you work things out."

"You're probably right." I waved the letter. "I'm embarrassed my mother had to do this. Give me a push from the grave just to go see my brother."

"Sometimes the people we love know us better than we know ourselves."

I nodded, thinking of what my son had said. "Cody told me I've been hiding."

"Hiding? From what?"

I shrugged. "He said I need to answer that question for myself."

Lisa hugged me with both arms this time, as she had when I was a child. And for a moment I felt like a girl wrapped in a mother's hug. "You need to go see your brother today. Before you chicken out," she said.

But I felt panic at the idea. "Now you sound like Mom," I said.

Lisa sat back. "How so?"

"She was always telling me how to live my life. She kept pushing me to do things I didn't want to do."

"She was your *mother*." Lisa shooed me away with both hands. "Now go. See your brother. Take him his yo-yo."

I grinned — the whole thing sounded so silly. "Okay, I'll go. I'll take Doug his damn yo-yo." I put the letter and yo-yo in the box and slipped it back into my purse. "But not now.

I've had enough emotion for one day. And I'm sure Doug is out with his buddies."

My aunt put her hand on my shoulder. "No, honey. You're not putting this visit off any longer. Today is the anniversary of your mother's death. You need to go see your brother *now*."

FIVE

WHEN DOUG OPENED his apartment door he looked surprised to see me. "Rhonda!" he said. "What are you doing here?"

"Can't a girl visit her brother?" I said.

"It's just been a while." He was dressed in plaid pajama bottoms and a T-shirt. His feet were bare. When he saw me glance at his outfit he said, "Sorry about my getup. I just got out of the shower. I planned on lounging around this evening."

"I hope you don't mind me just dropping in like this," I said.

"No, of course not. Come in."

He stepped back to let me enter and closed the door behind me. The kitchen and living room were one open space. Doug kept his weight set in the living room part. He didn't own a couch. Instead a recliner sat in front of the big-screen TV. There was an empty pizza box on the coffee table in front of the chair. Chip bags littered the floor around it.

As I followed him inside he picked up several pairs of socks from the floor. "Sorry about the mess," he said. "I wasn't expecting a visitor tonight." Or this week, I thought. He hadn't cleaned the place for several days. The room smelled stale, like old food and sweaty socks.

He dropped the socks in his chair. Then we stood in silence for a minute. Neither of us knew what to say. My brother looked nervous.

He was a handsome guy who had my mother's dark hair and eyes.

Finally, he asked, "Would you like something to drink?"

"No, I just had tea with Lisa."

"Oh, how is she doing?"

"Good," I said. "You haven't seen her recently?"

"No." He ran a hand through his wet hair. "I've been so busy."

"Me too."

"I gathered that. It's been, what, a year since we've seen each other?"

"Yes, at Mom's funeral," I said.

"I remember," he said. "But then, how could I forget? Look, was there a reason you dropped by?"

"Yes." I glanced around briefly for a place to sit, but there was only the one chair. "Maybe we should talk in the kitchen," I said.

"Sure."

The kitchen counter also served as a table in this small apartment. It was covered in dishes. Doug sat on a stool in front of it, but I couldn't take the mess. I stacked the dirty dishes and set them neatly in the sink.

"My housekeeper comes on Fridays," he said. "Tomorrow," he added.

"You don't have to apologize on my account," I said as I washed my hands.

"Really?" He nodded at the stack of dishes I had just put in the sink. "You were always such a neat freak."

"I like to be organized, that's all," I said.

"Remember that time I came home from vacation and you had cleaned my apartment? You organized my cupboards and everything. What the hell? You broke in here and cleaned up *my* place."

"I—I just couldn't stand it anymore," I said. "I'd thought you'd be pleased. But I did all that work for you, and you got angry at me for it." I brushed crumbs off the counter with my sleeve. "Anyway, I didn't break in. You had given me a key."

"Only so you could water my plants while I was away."

I sighed. I hadn't been here five minutes and we were already bickering. "I didn't come here to argue," I said.

"What *did* you come here for?"

I reached into my purse and pulled the old green yo-yo from the small box Mom had sent. "To give you this." Doug's eyes lit up as he took it from me.

"Where on earth did you find this?" he asked. "I thought I'd lost it for good."

"It came in the mail this morning." I paused. "Mom sent it."

"*Mom* sent it?"

"Well, not exactly. Before she passed away she arranged to have someone send it to me. And she must have asked that person to make sure it arrived today. You know what today is, right? It's exactly a year since Mom died."

"Seems like yesterday," he said.

I sat down on the stool next to him. "I know."

He held up the yo-yo. "Who really sent this?"

"I was hoping you could tell me," I said.

"How would I know?"

"At first I thought maybe Cody was responsible. I could see Mom talking him into sending a package for her. Then I thought maybe Lisa mailed it to me. She's more likely, don't you think? But they both claim they didn't put it in the mail."

"Why would Mom want my yo-yo mailed to you instead of to me?"

"The yo-yo came with instructions," I said. "From Mom." I pulled the letter out of the box. "She said I had to deliver the yo-yo to you in person."

Doug laughed. "Good old Mom. Always playing the peacemaker. Can I see the letter?"

I handed it to him and watched as he read it. "It's so weird," he said when he was done. "I could hear Mom's voice as I read it, clear as a bell." He grinned at me. "She was right, you know. You always got so mad when I tried to teach you anything."

I flicked a kernel of popcorn off the counter. "And you got mad at me when I said you needed to clean up your mess."

"Point taken."

I tapped the bottom of the letter. "Look how she signed off. She says, *That's it for now.* I half expect to hear from her again."

"Are you going to listen to Mom and let me teach you a trick or two?" Doug asked. He quickly looped the string over his fingers to do the Rock the Baby trick. The spinning yo-yo rocked back and forth in the triangle of string he held.

Then, just as quickly, he let go of the string. He dropped the yo-yo and did the Walk the Dog trick. The yo-yo "walked" or rolled across the floor while Doug held the string. It did look a little like he was walking a dog on a leash.

"I'm not sure teaching me yo-yo tricks was what she had in mind," I said.

"What do you suppose she did have in mind then? What else could I possibly teach *you*?"

"You're the oldest," I said. "You tell me." I waved at the beer bottles piled in a recycling bin in the corner. "How to party?"

"Maybe that's exactly what you need, to get out, have some fun."

"What's that supposed to mean?"

"Have you dated much since your divorce? It's been, what? Five years since you and Glen split?"

I crossed my arms. "Dating is hard when you're a single mom. Men aren't all that eager to take on a new family."

"I wasn't asking if you were looking for a husband. I was just wondering if you'd had any fun, gone out on the town. Have you thought of asking a few friends to join you for a girls' night out?"

"I'm not much for that kind of thing," I said. "Besides, who would I ask?"

"Then you *haven't* gotten out of the house," said Doug.

"I'm a *mom*," I said. "Cody is my focus. I don't have time for a social life."

"But soon he'll be in university. Then what?"

"Then — I don't know," I said.

Doug put a hand on my arm. "Glen has moved on. Why haven't you?"

That remark felt like a punch to my stomach. I snatched Mom's letter from his hand and stuffed it into my purse. "How's this for moving on?" I said. I stomped past the recliner and weight set and slammed the apartment door behind me as I left. Why did my brother always make me so mad? As I marched to the parking lot I figured out why. Because he was so often right.

Doug had left the apartment and was coming after me. He was still barefoot. "Come on, Sis," he called from the stairs as I reached my car. "Don't be like that. I was only saying you need to think about yourself for once."

"Like you?" I said. "All you do is think about yourself."

"That's not fair."

"Isn't it? Where were you when Mom was sick? I ran my business, looked after my kid and took care of Mom too." I waved at his apartment window and the gigantic TV I could see there. "While you hung out with my ex and ate pizza in front of your big-screen TV. Where were you when I needed help?"

My brother didn't have an answer to that.

I opened my car door and got inside, turning my back on my brother.

"Say hi to Cody for me, will you?" he called out. "I miss the kid." He paused. "I'd like to see him."

That deflated my anger. For the second time that day I felt bad about the distance between my brother and me. I knew our broken relationship was hurting not only me, but also my son. There had to be a way to get past the hard feelings between us. I turned, trying to think of something to say. But my brother had already gone back inside and closed the door.

SIX

THE NEXT MORNING, I tried to sneak into the post office early as the postal clerk sorted mail. I knew if Susan saw me, she would have questions about the package from my mother. After my argument with Doug, I wasn't in the mood to answer them. Unless there was another delivery-notice card, I was out of there.

I was in luck. Susan was still sorting mail in the back. I could hear her sliding bills and flyers into mailboxes on the other side of the wall as I opened my own.

But as I bent down to grab my mail, her face suddenly appeared on the other side of my mailbox. "Peek-a-boo!" she said and laughed.

I startled. "Susan!" I cried. "You scared me!"

"I'm not that funny-looking, am I?" She grinned. She wasn't, of course. Susan had a warm, welcoming face. Though she did look a little strange now. She had to bend over to look at me through the mailbox. Her face was almost upside down.

"Here," she said, sliding a wrapped chocolate into my mailbox. "You looked like you could use a little cheering up after I gave you that box from your mom."

I took her offering. "Thanks," I said. "I'm sorry about my tears yesterday. It was an emotional day."

"I can imagine." She crouched down to talk to me through the small opening. "Are you going to tell me what was in that box? You looked like you'd seen a ghost when you opened it. Then you rushed out of here."

"Oh, it was nothing."

"You're not fooling me. You get a package from your mother on the anniversary of her death. Then you open it and freak out. Whatever was in that box must have been pretty interesting."

I sighed. I wasn't getting out of this one. "She sent a letter and—" I paused—"a yo-yo."

Susan blinked. "I hear that right? A yo-yo?"

"It was my brother's yo-yo from when he was a kid."

"Why would Meg send you your brother's yo-yo?"

I unwrapped the chocolate and popped it in my mouth. I needed a moment to come up with something that would satisfy Susan and end the conversation. I didn't want to tell her about my family troubles.

When I didn't answer right away Susan waved at me through the narrow hole. "Come around to the counter. Talking to you through your mailbox is giving me a neck ache." She grinned and disappeared from view.

I closed and locked my mailbox. So much for avoiding Susan's questions. I quickly sorted through my mail, looking for another delivery notice. I both hoped and feared my mother had sent another package. But there wasn't one. I tossed the flyers in the recycling bin and went to the counter.

Susan was waiting for me. She was dressed in her post-office uniform, as always. Her unruly hair was bunched into a messy bun.

"Why did she send a yo-yo?" she asked again. "Did she explain?"

"She wanted me to deliver the yo-yo to my brother in person."

Susan lifted her chin, understanding. "Meg said she hoped you two would find a way to patch things up."

"Mom told you about *that*?"

"She said you and Doug had grown apart. She figured it had something to do with your ex-husband. What's his name? Glen? I understand your brother and your ex are old friends."

"Sounds like my mom told you a lot about my life. Maybe too much."

Susan shrugged. "She was worried for you, especially since she knew she didn't have long to live. She didn't want you to be alone after she passed on."

"I am *not* alone. I have my son."

"I didn't mean to offend you," she said. "We all need family." She leaned over the counter. "Did you take Doug the yo-yo?"

I stepped back. "Yes, I did, as a matter of fact."

"And?" She waved to get me to spill the beans, to tell her what happened. "Did you and your brother hash things out?"

"I don't think that's any of your business."

I figured that rude response would stop Susan from asking more questions. Instead she laughed. I hated that. My mom had laughed when I got mad at her. It made me feel like my anger was silly. Maybe it was. Mom always told me I was too sensitive. I was easily hurt.

"I take it your visit with your brother didn't go well," Susan said.

I looked at my feet. "No," I mumbled. "Doug and I just ended up arguing again." I threw up both hands, annoyed with myself as much as him. "Every time I'm with my brother, I act like a stupid kid again. He does too. It's like we're still a couple of teens, fighting over things that don't really matter."

"Huh." Susan put a hand to her chin. "I've had similar problems with my sister. Can I tell you something Meg once told me?"

"I guess."

"Your mom said when we're with family, it's like we're in a play onstage. We're actors stuck in whatever role we grew up playing. Even when we're adults and have changed, we still act like the kids we once were. And we don't really see our family members for who they are now. We see them as who they once were, when we were growing up."

I thought about that. It made sense. "So, with Doug, I still feel like the youngest. I'm always trying to prove myself to him. I resent him when he offers me advice. And I hate it when he embarrasses me."

"I wonder how he sees you?"

"As bossy," I said. "Always messing with his stuff."

"Do you see yourself that way?"

"No, not really. He got mad at me once when I cleaned up his apartment. But I was just trying to help him out."

"Did he really need your help? I doubt Doug sees himself the way you do. Maybe it's time you got to know each other as you are now, as adults."

I shook my head. "That isn't going to happen. If I see him again, we'll argue. My visit with him yesterday was a disaster."

"One of you is going to have to be the first to apologize. Sounds like your mom was asking you to be that person."

I crossed my arms. "I'm not saying sorry to Doug," I said. "I have nothing to apologize for. He abandoned me after my divorce. He embarrassed me at Mom's funeral. And he should have helped me out when Mom was sick."

Susan raised her eyebrows. "Well, I expect it will take time to patch things up with your brother."

"Have you finished sorting the parcels?" I asked to change the subject.

"Hoping for another package from Meg?" Susan smiled, but kindly.

"I guess," I said. "In the letter Mom seemed to suggest there would be another. As she signed off she said, *That's it for now*."

"Let me check."

I drummed my fingers on the counter as I waited for Susan. I heard her rummaging in the back. Finally, she came out, empty-handed. "Nope, sorry. Nothing today."

My shoulders drooped. I was disappointed. I had hoped to hear from my mother again.

Susan put a hand on my arm. "Rhonda, I'm sorry if I pushed too hard. You're right. All this is a private matter. Meg was a dear friend. And I know you meant the world to her. I just want to see you happy."

Her hand felt warm and comforting. I again understood why my mother had liked

Susan. She had a relaxed way about her. She *was* nosy, and she did know too much about my life. But I also felt strangely comfortable around her. I rarely opened up to strangers, yet I had told her all about my brother.

"It's okay," I said. "I just wish Mom would have kept all this to herself. It's embarrassing to have a stranger know so much about me."

Susan seemed hurt by that remark. She pulled back. "I understand," she said. Her tone of voice became more formal. "If another package arrives, I'll get a delivery-notice card into your box right away."

"I doubt there will be anything else from Mom," I said. "I should feel lucky that she thought to send me one last letter."

Then my cell phone rang. I glanced at the incoming number. Lisa. I stepped away from the counter to answer the call. "Hello?"

"Rhonda, can you come over after work?" My aunt sounded excited.

I hesitated. It was a half-hour drive into town. "I was over there yesterday."

"It's important." She paused. "I'm at the post office right now. I just received a letter in the mail. It's from Meg."

"From Mom?"

"She asked me to invite you over. And you *must* bring Cody with you."

"Okay," I said. "We'll be there about five-thirty. But why is it so important to bring Cody?"

"You'll see."

SEVEN

WHEN CODY AND I arrived at Lisa's door, she immediately hugged my son. "I wonder if you can do me a favor," she asked him. "There's a guitar case in the attic. Can you grab it for me?" Cody nodded and ran up the stairs. "It's just inside the attic door," Lisa called after him. "The light switch is on the right." Then she turned back to me, her eyes sparkling.

"What are you up to?" I asked.

"Come in!" She closed the door behind me and led me to the kitchen. We both sat at the table. "A month before Meg died she called me over and insisted I take her guitar. I had never learned how to play. I wasn't interested. So, I put the guitar in the attic, and it's been collecting dust ever since."

My son bounded back down the stairs, carrying the guitar case. He slid it onto the kitchen counter to open it. There was a beautiful guitar inside.

Lisa pulled a letter from her pocket and waved it at me. "Then I got this letter from your mother this morning." She turned to Cody. "Meg wanted you to have this guitar," she said. "She asked me to give it to you."

Cody's face lit up. "Are you serious?" he asked. "It's a high-end Gibson. You know how expensive these guitars are?" He lifted the guitar from the case. "I can really keep this?"

"It's yours! Just take it outside to play right now, okay? I'd like to have a quick chat with your mother."

We both watched Cody carry the guitar through the sliding glass doors to the deck. He spent several minutes tuning the guitar and then started to play.

"Your mother had another, bigger favor to ask of me," Lisa told me. "But I want to see what you think before I agree to it." She hesitated before handing me the letter from my mother. I read it.

Dear Lisa:

I'm writing this letter just after your visit. Remember the guitar I gave you? That was only moments ago for me, but a year ago for you. You looked confused when I gave it to you, as we both know you don't play. But the guitar isn't really for you. Please give it to Cody. Now, as I write, I don't think he's quite ready for an instrument of this quality. But by the time you receive this letter, he will have matured enough to take good care of it.

Do you know he practices every day? I've been impressed that he stuck with his lessons this long. He will go on to teach music down the road, I'm sure of it. Make sure he gets this guitar, will you?

I have another favor to ask. Cody may be a young man now, but he still needs a grandmother. He will for some time. Will you be that for him, now that I'm gone?

I think he can offer you quite a bit in return. I know you always wanted children of your own. Being a grandmother is even more fun! No need to train the kid. That's Mom's job. As a grandmother, you can just enjoy your time with him! And maybe that will inspire Rhonda to spend more time with you.

That's it for now.

You were always so very dear to me, Lisa. Be good to yourself.

I'll love you always.
Hugs and kisses,
Meg

I stared at the letter for a moment, taking it in. Then I folded it and gave it back to my aunt. "She wants you to be a grandmother to Cody."

Lisa nodded.

"Is that something *you* want?"

"Yes! But I figured I needed to ask your permission first."

"Lisa, you don't need my consent."

She paused. "You haven't visited much recently, so I wasn't sure —" She stopped there.

Lisa and I didn't have the kind of strained relationship my brother and I had. Still, my mother was right. I hadn't visited my aunt nearly as much as I should have.

"I'm so sorry I haven't been around much," I said. "To be honest, I'm not sure why I haven't gotten out more. But I do know it wasn't anything to do with you. Cody and I drive into town every Saturday to shop. Can we pop in on you then?"

"I'd love that." She wiped a tear from the corner of her eye. It occurred to me that Lisa might be as lonely as I was. Why *hadn't* I visited her more?

"Cody buses into town for school," I said. "On some Fridays he can walk here after school and stay overnight. I can pick him up the next day."

"That would be great! We can watch zombie movies together."

I laughed. "I didn't know that was your thing."

Lisa winked. "I suspect there's a lot we don't know about each other."

"You're probably right."

"Tea?"

"Please."

Lisa poured us both a cup and then blew over her tea before taking a sip. "How did things go with your brother?" she asked.

I sighed. "Not so good. Doug and I just started arguing about the same old things."

"You *are* going to see him again, though, right?"

"Not anytime soon," I said. "I'm not sure what I'd say."

We were both silent for a moment, listening to Cody play his guitar.

I put down my cup. "You know, I just don't get Mom," I said. "She could have given Cody that guitar before she died. Instead she made a production out of giving it to you. And she sends me the yo-yo to give to Doug. If she really wanted Doug and me to mend things, why didn't she just say something before she died?"

"She did, remember? Before she got sick she asked you to sort out things with your brother. You got angry at her, told her to stop meddling in your affairs." My aunt paused. "I think you're angry with her now."

"No, I'm not!" I said. Then I thought about it. "Okay, yes, I am angry." I picked up the letter Mom had sent Lisa and waved it. "She's manipulating me, pulling my strings, even from the grave."

"How so?"

I paused as I came up with a way to explain. "When I was a kid Mom tried to get me to audition for school plays even though she knew I was terrified of being onstage. I'm mad because she's doing that again here."

"Because she's pushing you to heal old hurts between you and Doug, you mean? Are you sure that's why you're angry at her?"

"Why else would I be mad?"

"Maybe because she got sick and you had to take care of her."

"That's not it at all," I said. "It was my job to take care of her. I was her daughter."

"And yet you're mad at Doug because he didn't help."

"I had to juggle work, being a mom to Cody *and* taking care of Mom. I was exhausted. Doug is a single guy. He didn't help at all."

"That may be true. But are you mad at Doug for not helping or at your Mom for getting sick and leaving you?"

"You can't get mad at someone for getting sick and dying."

"Can't you?"

I took sip of tea as I thought about that. "If I'm mad at Mom at all, it's because she told Susan everything about me."

"Susan?"

"The postal clerk at my post office."

Lisa lifted her chin. "Oh, right, Susan."

"You've met her? You don't use that post office."

"I was in there a few times with your mother. Meg and Susan were great friends."

"A little too friendly, I think."

"You can hardly fault your mother for that."

"I can when she tells everyone about my life."

"Oh, Rhonda. Meg didn't tell *everyone* about your life, only people she trusted. In many ways, she was as shy and private as you."

"She wore a wedding dress to my graduation ceremony!"

"At least she dyed it purple first." Lisa laughed, and I found myself chuckling with her.

"Mom always had to be the center of attention," I said. "I would hardly call that shy."

"Being onstage was her way of getting over her shyness. Did you know she didn't talk until she was four? It wasn't that she *couldn't* talk. She was simply too shy to open her mouth. I did the talking for her."

"I find that very hard to believe."

"It's true! Then in fifth grade she had a teacher who urged her to take a part in the school Christmas play. It was just a small acting role, but she had to recite a few lines. She didn't want to. More to the point, she was scared just like you were. But she did it. And something changed for her. After that she pushed *herself* to do things she was afraid of. She took on bigger and bigger parts in the school plays, until she ended up in lead roles."

Lisa took my hand. "But she never stopped being afraid. That shy little girl who was too frightened to talk was always a part of her. She simply learned to face her fears." She squeezed my hand. "That's what she was trying to do for you when she made you deliver that yo-yo to Doug. She was helping you get over your fears so you would go see your brother. Go see him again."

I pulled my hand from hers. "I just can't," I said. "There's too much hurt there."

"If you can't talk to Doug about what's bugging you without getting mad, maybe you and Doug can just spend time together. The three of you could take Cody to the go-kart track like you used to."

I sat back and crossed my arms. I didn't like *anyone* telling me what to do, not even Lisa.

Lisa studied me for a moment and then topped up my tea. "Maybe you can't heal things for yourself," she said as she poured. "But you're a good mom. I know you can do it for Cody."

She put down the teapot and nodded at my son. Cody was still playing his guitar on the other side of the glass doors. If I let him, he'd play that thing all night.

"His dad isn't in the picture like he used to be," Lisa said. "Cody may need a grandma, but I think he needs an uncle more."

EIGHT

CODY STAYED WITH Lisa that night to watch a zombie movie with her. I went home alone. The house seemed so empty. I watched a dumb space movie on TV and still felt lonely. And when I heard a knock on the door, I was startled.

I clicked off the TV and opened the front door just a crack to find my brother standing on the doorstep. He held a box and was dressed in a light jacket and jeans. That night

I was the one in pajamas, flannel ones with kitty paw prints. And I wore the happy-face slippers my mother had given me. I knew I looked ridiculous. I opened the door all the way anyway.

"Hey," Doug said.

I crossed my arms. "Cody isn't here. He's staying at Lisa's tonight."

"I'm here to see you, actually."

"Oh?"

"This came in the mail today." He offered me the box and I took it. It had a bit of weight to it.

"Let me guess," I said. "No return address?"

Doug nodded. "Mom included a note with it. She told me to give the box to you." He hesitated. "Well, I'll leave you to open it." He turned and started to walk toward his truck.

"Wait," I said.

He turned back. I pointed a thumb back at the house. "Come in for a soda?"

"I'm not sure that's a good idea."

"I'd like you here while I open this." I held up the box. "I *know* Mom would have wanted you here."

"You're right. She did." My brother stepped inside.

I placed the box on the kitchen table and opened it. Inside there was yet another box. It was covered in red velvet, and when I opened it a ballerina popped up. The tiny doll twirled around as music started playing. My dad had given me this jewelry box on my twelfth birthday, just before he passed away.

"I didn't know Mom still had this," I said.

"It looks like she kept a lot of our things after we moved out."

I looked up at my brother. "Did Mom say anything about this in the letter?"

"Read it for yourself." My brother handed me the single page of writing paper.

Oh, my darling boy!

I hope you don't mind that I still think of you as my boy. It startles me sometimes to see you all grown up. But, of course, you've been a man for many years now. And what a fine man you are. I hope you know that.

By now Rhonda has brought you that old green yo-yo. When you were ten, you never went anywhere without it! Then it was a trophy you kept on your bookshelf. Later it sat forgotten on your windowsill until you moved out. But I kept it as a reminder of those hours I watched you do yo-yo tricks on the porch.

Even if Rhonda won't let you teach her those tricks now, show Cody a few, will you? I know he'd love that.

In this package you'll find your sister's music box. You already know what I'm about to ask. Please deliver it to her in person. I'm fairly sure the yo-yo wasn't enough to do the trick, but maybe this music box will get you two talking? I hope so.

*If not, please keep trying. Eventually you'll settle
your differences. Rhonda is stubborn, but she will
come around.*

    I love you, son, and I always will.
    Hugs and kisses,
    Mom

The tinkling song on the music box wound
down as I finished reading. I looked up at my
brother. "Am I really that stubborn?" I asked.

Doug took the letter from me. "Sometimes." He thought about it. "Maybe stubborn
isn't the right word. You have trouble changing
gears, getting over things."

"You're no different. You dig your heels in
too."

"I know." He pocketed the letter. "Mom
really wanted us to work things out, didn't she?"

I laughed a little. "She sure did."

"Then I guess it's time we did." He pulled
out a chair and sat at the table.

I hesitated a moment and then got us each a can of soda from the fridge. After I joined him we sat at the table for several minutes, not knowing what to say. To fill the silence, I wound up the music box. The ballerina twirled again.

"I used to dance to this music in my room," I said. "In my mind, I was this tiny ballerina."

"You always stopped dancing when I came into the room."

I closed the lid on the ballerina and the music ended. "I guess I was shy," I said. "Nothing like Mom."

"When you were really little, you weren't shy at all."

"What are you talking about?"

"Mom dropped you off at preschool before she took me to school. Sometimes I was there when you did show and tell. You most often got up and danced."

"No, I didn't."

"Yes, you did! You wore your ballerina outfit, your pink tutu, every day. Mom couldn't get you to wear anything else. You wanted to be a dancer when you grew up."

Like most little girls, I imagined. "Mom must have liked that," I said. "She always wanted to see me onstage. Instead I turned out to be a bookkeeper."

"Mom was proud of you."

I shook my head. "When I started out in this business, she asked me if I was sure I wanted to keep books. She said bookkeeping was boring."

"No. I remember that conversation. Mom said she was worried that you would find bookkeeping boring. You were an active kid, always moving. She thought you needed a job where you were up and about."

"Really? I've been mad at Mom all these years over that. I thought she didn't accept my job choice."

Doug shrugged. "She only wanted you to be happy in your work. When she saw that you were, she was happy too."

I stretched my legs. "She was right when she said I needed to move. I can't sit for long. I go on several walks a day."

"Have you thought of taking yoga classes? I noticed there's a yoga studio right behind your post office. I just got back into weights myself because the gym is a good place to meet friends." He grinned. "Or find a date."

"I doubt I'll find a date at a yoga class." I said. "Likely all middle-aged women. But I'll check it out anyway."

We sat in silence again.

Finally, Doug said, "Look, do you even remember why you were mad at me?"

I stared at him like he should know.

"I understand I should have helped out more when Mom was sick. I just couldn't stand to see her like that, you know?"

I nodded. I had watched my mother waste away.

"Does that make me a coward?" Doug asked.

"I *had* to be there for her."

"I guess I should have been too."

"Yeah, you should have," I said.

Doug held up the letter. "Mom wasn't mad at me. Why are you?"

I glanced at him and away.

"Or are you mad because I was still friends with Glen after you guys divorced?"

"Look, I get it," I said. "Glen was your friend for a long time. Before he and I met."

"Since we were teens."

"But *I'm* your sister."

"You thought I had to choose between you."

"You *did* choose. After our divorce, you spent time with Glen but not with me."

"That's not true."

"Isn't it?"

He sat back and stared at the ceiling for a moment. "Maybe I did pull away from you after your divorce."

"From both me *and* Cody."

"But Rhonda, you did too."

I took a deep breath to control my anger and then nodded slowly. "You're right."

Doug leaned forward again, clasping his hands together on the table. "The truth is, I was uncomfortable," he said. "I felt caught between you and Glen. You were both so angry at each other. If I visited you, you said stuff about Glen. If I visited Glen, he said stuff about you. I stopped hanging out with both of you."

"You did? I mean, I thought you and Glen were still friends."

"He comes over now and again, but I rarely see him."

I sat back in my chair. "Then why didn't you visit us? Cody misses you."

"I miss him too. I miss being around family, you know? I even miss Mom's horrible Sunday dinners."

I put a hand to my mouth. "Oh god, she overcooked everything."

"Her pot roast was so dry!"

"And her peas!"

"Mush!"

"Like eating pablum," I said. "Green baby food."

We both laughed.

"But at least I got to see you all every week. Now—" He turned his can of soda. "I don't have many friends either, you know."

I thought of the single chair in his living room, stuck in front of the ridiculously large television. I'm sure he didn't have a girlfriend either. If he did, he'd own a couch. My brother was as lonely as I was, maybe lonelier. At least I had Cody.

"Let's have one of those horrible family

dinners on Sunday," I said. "Right here. I'll invite Lisa over."

"As long as you don't let her near the oven. She overcooks everything just like Mom did."

I laughed again. "I'll do the cooking," I said.

He nodded. "Then I'll bring dessert."

"I don't suppose you have your yo-yo with you this evening?"

My brother grinned. "No."

"Maybe you could bring it over to our house on Sunday. After dinner you could show Cody and me a few tricks. Deal?"

He nodded. "Deal. So, are we good?"

"Not yet," I said. "But we'll get there."

NINE

ON SUNDAY, IN honor of Mom, I cooked a pot roast with potatoes and green peas. But I didn't overcook them like Mom always did. Cody and Doug sat on one side of the table, talking about guitars and cars. Lisa and I on sat on the other side, chatting about our clients. The conversation rolled around to the packages Mom had sent the past week.

"I'm still wondering about Mom's timing," I said. "Why did she send those packages *now*?

Why a year after her death? Why didn't she have them delivered right after the funeral?"

"Or before," Doug said. "She could have just handed her gifts to us. Talked to us in person."

Lisa helped herself to more roast. "I expect she knew you needed time to heal," she said. She glanced at my brother and then me. "Both of you were very emotional in Meg's final weeks. You directed your grief at each other. Remember that fight you two had in the kitchen at the funeral reception?"

"You really had it out," Cody said. "Everyone in the church heard."

I felt my face flush. My behavior at the funeral embarrassed me now. "But how did Mom know we would still be distant from each other a year after her death?" I asked.

"She knew her kids, that's how," said Lisa. She cut into the beef. "She knew neither of you was likely to make the first move. With those packages she gave you two an excuse to talk."

"Your ugly green yo-yo," I said to Doug.

"And your girly music box." He stood and twirled like a ballerina. We laughed.

I gestured at the bread basket, and Cody handed it to me. "There's one last thing bothering me," I said.

Cody grinned. "Like, who mailed the packages for Grandma a year after she died?"

"Exactly," I said, pointing a breadstick in his direction.

Cody held up both hands. "Don't look at me," he said. "I had nothing to do with it."

"I believe you. You're not organized enough to pull this off." I turned to my aunt. "Lisa, don't you think it's time you confessed? You and Mom planned all this, didn't you? *You* mailed those packages."

Lisa shook her head as she finished chewing. "Wasn't me," she said.

I gave her a playful punch in the arm. "Come on," I said. "We know it was you."

"Seriously, it wasn't me," she said. "I'm as baffled as you are."

I turned to my brother. "Doug?"

"You really think *I'm* organized enough to pull this off?"

"I guess not."

"Who then?" asked Cody. "Was it you, Mom? Did you send those packages?"

"Me?" I put a hand to my chest. "God, no."

Doug laughed. "Are you kidding? Rhonda wouldn't have come over to see me if Mom hadn't made her."

I stuck out my tongue at him.

"Maybe one of Grandma's friends sent the parcels then?" Cody asked. "A teacher from the school maybe?"

Lisa held her wineglass up. "Whoever it was, let's raise a glass to them. To the mystery person who is responsible for this dinner.

She, or he, brought us all together."

"Under Mom's direction," I said.

"Here's to Mom!" Doug said.

"Yes, to Meg," said my aunt.

We clicked our glasses together.

AFTER SUPPER LISA and I put the leftovers away as Doug and Cody hung out in the living room. Lisa nudged me, and we both watched Doug show Cody how to do the Walk the Dog yo-yo trick. "See, I was right," said Lisa. "I knew you could fix things with your brother if you had the right motivation. You invited Doug over for Cody, didn't you?"

"And for myself. I missed him too. This dinner was for all of us. Let's make it a regular event, okay?"

"You got it. But you shouldn't have to cook every time. We'll take turns. I'll host it at my place next Sunday."

"Um…okay." I thought of Lisa's cooking. Doug was right. Lisa overcooked everything just like Mom had. "I don't mind helping you make dinner," I said.

She laughed. "Don't like my cooking, eh?"

"I didn't say that."

"Your mom and I were never great cooks," she said. "We'd get distracted and burn whatever we had in the oven. How about we order in next week. I'm sure Cody and Doug wouldn't turn down pizza."

I watched Lisa put the bowl of leftover peas in the fridge. She had brought her pink bunny slippers with her to wear in my house. Mom had done that. She had even taken slippers to school. Her slippers were always goofy, shaped like cartoon characters or animals. Her last pair had been in the shape of moose heads.

"You know, Lisa," I said, "you *are* a lot like Mom."

She laughed. "*I'm* like Meg?" she said. "Have you looked in the mirror lately?" Lisa took me by the shoulders and turned me to face the mirror hanging by the kitchen door. "If anyone is like Meg, it's you."

I took a look at myself. For once I had worn something other than gray sweats and a hoodie. I had searched the back of my closet and pulled out a bright blue blouse for the evening. I'd even put on makeup and tamed my hair.

Lisa was right. I not only looked like my mother, but also shared many of her traits. Like her, I was both stubborn and shy. Maybe I could use my stubbornness to get over some of my fears, as my mom had.

But then, my brother was also a lot like Mom. Not just in his looks, but in his sense of humor. I even saw my mother in my son. He had her eyes, and her determination, her willpower. I knew he would spend his life in the arts just like she had. I saw my mother in all the people closest to me. Maybe I hadn't lost her after all.

I glanced back at my brother and son through the mirror. I could see them in the living room behind me, playing with the yo-yo. Doug was now teaching Cody the Rock the Baby trick. I grinned — they both seemed to be enjoying themselves so much. Then, just for a moment, I thought I saw my mother too. She stood behind them in the dark corner, smiling. But when I turned away from the mirror to look at her directly, she was gone.

TEN

MONDAY WAS A beautiful June morning, the kind of morning that always puts a spring in my step. Not a cloud in the sky. I breathed in the scent of the wild roses as I walked down for the mail. I felt better than I'd felt in a long time.

Susan wasn't at the counter when I came into the post office. I was surprised to feel disappointed at that. Only the week before she had just been a clerk to me. Now I had started to think of her as a friend.

There was even less mail than usual this day. But there *was* a delivery-notice card. Had I received another package from my mother? I hurried to the counter to find out.

Susan came out from the back moments later, carrying a box. She handed it to me. "How did you know—?" I asked.

"I saw you coming in and knew you had something waiting." She peered down at the box. "Another mystery package? I see it has no return address."

"It's from my mother."

"Well, open it!"

I didn't hesitate. I tore off the brown wrapping. But I was disappointed to find there was no letter from my mother, only another box. Like the one it had come in, it was also covered in brown paper wrapping. Across the top my mother had written *For Susan*.

Puzzled, I pulled the second box out of

the first. "It's for you!" I said, handing the postal clerk the box.

"Me? How can it be for me?"

"You're the only Susan I know. You and my mother *were* friends."

"Yes, but —"

I offered her the box. "Then this must be for you."

Susan took the box from me. This time *she* looked like she was about to cry.

"Well, open it!" I said, echoing her.

Susan used a letter opener to carefully open the brown wrapping. Then she folded it neatly and put it to the side. She was being *too* neat and tidy — like me, I thought.

"Oh, for heaven's sake," I said. "Open the damn box!"

Susan laughed at my impatience. "Okay, okay!" She ripped off the tape and opened the flaps. Then she pulled out a wad of tissue paper. Inside were a delicate teacup and saucer.

"That's one of Mom's teacups," I said. "I know the pattern. I have the matching teapot and cups to go with it at home."

"Then you should have it," Susan said, offering it to me.

"No, it's yours. Mom gave it to you."

Inside the cup there was a folded sheet of writing paper. Susan opened it. "It *is* from your mother," she said.

"Read it! I want to hear what it says."

Susan lifted the glasses that hung around her neck and put them on. She hesitated a moment and then read the letter out loud.

"Dear Susan:

By now my daughter has likely figured out that it was you who delivered my little packages to my family. I hope our plan worked and that Rhonda and Doug are in each other's lives again.

This cup is a gift to say thank you for helping

me make that happen. Obviously, since I'm dead, I couldn't have done it without you!

I think you know why I chose to give you one of my teacups. Every day when I came in for the mail we had a lovely long talk. And every day we said we should get together for a visit over a cup of tea. But, well, we never did. Still, I enjoyed our friendship so very much.

I have one last favor to ask of you. I gave Rhonda the teapot and cups that match this one. Bring this cup up to her place, will you? And have that cup of tea with my daughter. I think you may find that you have even more in common with Rhonda than you had with me. You're nearly the same age, for one thing. And you've both had a few hard years. Rhonda could use a friend, and I suspect you could too.

Give my daughter a hug for me, will you? I miss you both so very much.

Hugs and kisses,

Meg"

Susan didn't look up at me right away. She fiddled with the letter.

"*You* sent all those packages?" I asked.

"For your mother," Susan said. "This was all her idea. Mostly. She asked me not to tell you."

"Why, that sly old woman. I can't believe my mother would trick me like this. And you helped her!"

Susan peered at me over her glasses like she thought I was about to lose it.

Then I laughed. "But I'm so glad she did."

"You are?"

"Yesterday I had the first Sunday dinner with my family in a year. My brother, Doug, and my aunt Lisa came over. I almost felt like Mom was there too. I hadn't realized how much my son, Cody, missed being around family." I picked up the teacup. "Or how much I had."

Susan grinned, relieved. "Oh, thank God!"

"My mom wants us to have tea, does she?"

Susan waved a hand. For once *she* looked embarrassed. "We don't have to do that. I wouldn't want to impose. I know I'm just a stranger to you."

I handed her the cup and saucer. "I'm so very sorry I was rude to you on Friday. I've come in here for years, and you've always been friendly to me. I could have invited you over for tea years ago, but I didn't."

"I understand."

I shook my head. "No, it's time I started letting people back into my life."

"I know exactly what you mean. I lost my husband a few years ago in a car accident. Work and kids were everything for a while."

"Oh!" I said. "I had no idea."

"Your mom helped me through that tough time, just like she helped you."

"Then let's have that cup of tea at my place. You can tell me all about it, in a more private setting."

"Sometime next week?" she asked.

"How about today, after your shift? I'm not putting things off anymore. When I do that, they just don't happen."

"Okay. I'll pop up to your place right after closing." Susan slipped around the counter to join me. "But there is one more delivery from your mom, remember?"

"What's that?"

"This." Susan wrapped her arms around me and gave me that one last big hug from my mom.

AUTHOR'S NOTE

No Return Address was inspired by my own
Canada Post story. Continuing a tradition from
childhood, my mother gave my sisters and me
an Advent calendar every Christmas. Mom did
this even after we were grown and had families
of our own. The Advent calendar my mother
mailed to me always arrived at my rural post
office at the end of November.

In the spring of 2007 my mother passed
away. As you can imagine, our family grieved for
her all that year. When December approached
I felt a new wave of sadness as I walked to the
post office. I knew I would never receive another
Advent calendar from my mother.

But when I opened my post box, there
was a delivery notice waiting as usual. And
when I took that notice to the postal clerk, she
handed me a package with a shape I recognized

immediately. I pulled the brown paper off and there it was, my Advent calendar.

There was no note. For just a moment I wondered, could Mom have sent this? No, of course she couldn't have. And then it occurred to me to look at the return address on the wrapping. My oldest sister had sent me the Advent calendar. She continues to do so every Christmas.

And there you'll find the idea behind this short novel. A mysterious package arrives in the mail, bringing with it a voice from the past. In this case, though, the sender is someone who has passed away. In trying to figure out how this is possible, the woman who receives the parcel finds it is a bigger gift than she could ever imagine.

I hope the story will inspire you to send your own letter to family or friends. Perhaps, as it was for the character in this book, that letter will be the first step toward a reunion.

ACKNOWLEDGMENTS

I offer my heartfelt thanks to my oldest sister, who sends me an Advent calendar every Christmas. That act of kindness is the seed that sprouted into this short novel.

Check out the *National Post* story titled "Canada Post takes 45 years to deliver letter to Calgary woman living just 215 kilometres away from sender." You'll find it on the *National Post* website.

For a discussion on why brother-and-sister relationships are so important, go to the *Globe and Mail* website article "Adult siblings are seeking therapy together to heal old wounds and to strengthen their bond."

Here's to our brothers and sisters and the impact they have on our lives. May we keep them close.

By the age of eighteen, **Gail Anderson-Dargatz** knew she wanted to write about women in rural settings. Today Gail is a bestselling author. *A Recipe for Bees* and *The Cure for Death by Lightning* were finalists for the Scotiabank Giller Prize. She also teaches other authors how to write fiction. Gail lives in the Shuswap region of British Columbia. For more information, visit gailanderson-dargatz.ca.

Preview of *From Scratch* by
Gail Anderson-Dargatz

9781459815025 · $9.95 PB

I BRUSHED FLOUR off my apron as I stepped away from the kitchen area and up to the bakery counter to serve Murray. He was a widower a few years older than me, in his early forties. He still dressed like a construction worker even though he owned his own antique business now. He sold old dishes, toys and art online, through his website. "You know what I'm here for," he said, grinning.

I did. Murray turned up at the end of my morning shift almost every day. He always ordered the same thing. I handed him a cup of coffee and two oatmeal "doilies." I called these cookies doilies because as they baked, the dough spread out into crisp circles. They looked like the lace doilies people put under vases to protect their furniture.

"Thanks, Cookie," Murray said as he took the plate. He was the one who gave me the nickname Cookie. Now every regular at the bakery called me that. My real name is Eva.

"You ever going to give me the recipe so I can make these cookies at home?" he asked me.

I shook my head as I smiled shyly at him. We didn't use packaged mixes at this bakery. We baked everything from scratch. I made these cookies from my own recipe.

"Probably better if you don't tell me," he said. "I want a reason to keep coming in here." Murray held my gaze just a little too long, as if he liked me. But I wasn't sure. More to the point, I found it hard to believe he *could* be interested in me. He was such a handsome and accomplished man, with a business of his own.

And me? I just worked here, at this bakery. My hair was tucked in a hairnet because I'd been baking that morning. My apron was covered in flour and butter stains. I never wore makeup to work because it got so hot around the big commercial ovens. I always worked up a sweat. If I did wear mascara, it smudged. What could Murray possibly see in me?

Diana elbowed me as Murray went to his usual table by the window. "Like he needs another reason to come in here," she said. "He's got you."

She grinned at me, but I tried to ignore her. I wiped the counter to hide my embarrassment.

Diana was the owner of the bakery. She was in her sixties now and had owned the bakery-café in this strip mall for more than twenty-five years. The café looked a little dated too. The place could have used some fresh paint and new tables. But the big windows filled the space with light, and the room always smelled of sweet baked goods. The bakery-café was a favorite hangout, the only place to meet for coffee in this rural area just outside of town.

I had worked at the bakery since my daughter Katie was little. Katie had worked here summers as a teen. Now she took cooking courses at the college in town. But I had never gone to school to learn how to bake. I had learned all that from Diana, on the job. Then I practiced baking at home, making up my own recipes.

"Come on, Eva, when are you going to do something about that?" Diana asked me, nodding at Murray.

"What?" I asked, as if I didn't know.

"He likes you. And I *know* you like him."

I felt my face heat up. Were my feelings for Murray that obvious? "Murray is only being kind," I said.

"You don't give yourself enough credit," Diana said. "Your cookies are truly wonderful, but you're the reason Murray comes in here every morning. I see him watching you when you aren't looking."

He glanced up now to see us watching *him*. Caught, he quickly looked away.

"I don't have time for romance," I said. "I've got a kid, and I've got work. That's more than enough to fill my day."

"Katie is a grown woman now," said Diana. "She's in college. It's time to start thinking about yourself."

"Katie is still living at home. On top of paying for rent and food, I have to pay for her tuition now, the cost of her schooling. After I pay the bills on payday, I have hardly anything left over." I stopped when I saw the look on Diana's face. "I don't mean to complain," I said. "You've been good to me, letting me work overtime when I need the cash."

Diana sighed. "I wish I could give you even more hours, for my sake as well as yours." She rubbed her sore knee. She was about to have an operation on that knee. Standing on her feet for hours each day year after year had taken its toll on her. She looked tired and often winced in pain. "But with the economy the way it is…" She didn't finish her sentence.

I knew things had been hard for her and everyone in the community. When the small department store in this rural strip mall had closed down, one business after another had also closed. But, as Diana often said, people had to eat. There were enough regular customers, like Murray, to keep the bakery going. Even so, I knew Diana had been trying to sell the business so she could retire. The For Sale sign had been up outside the bakery for over a year. Diana had told me she would make sure the new owner kept me on, however. She would make it clear I helped her run the place.

Diana took my hand in hers. "Listen, Eva, since we're on the subject—" She hesitated.

"What is it?"

"I've been meaning to talk to you, not just about your hours, but about your job."

"My job?" I felt my stomach knot.

"As you know, I haven't had any serious offers on the bakery. No one wants to take the place on, not with all these other businesses in the mall shutting down. And I have my knee operation coming up."

She looked around the small bakery-café. The glass counter was full of baked goods. A row of small tables lined the windows. The place smelled of the cinnamon buns baking in the big oven in the kitchen behind us. "I've decided to close the bakery at the end of next month."

I covered my mouth. "Oh no!" I said.

"The tourists will be gone by then," she said. "Labor Day weekend is coming up. Summer is already just about over. I can't keep the place open any longer. I'll have to stay off this knee for several months after the operation."

"I understand," I said. I was sad for Diana — and for our customers. Without this bakery, there would be no place for people in the community to meet. They would have to drive into town just to go out for a cup of coffee. But I was most worried about myself and my daughter. What was I going to do without this job?